PEYTON MANNING
MOST VALUABLE QUARTERBACK

PERCY LEED

LERNER PUBLICATIONS ◆ MINNEAPOLIS

SCORE BIG with sports fans, reluctant readers, and report writers!

Lerner Sports is a database of high-interest biographies profiling notable sports superstars. Packed with fascinating facts, these bios explore the backgrounds, career-defining moments, and everyday lives of popular athletes. Lerner Sports is perfect for young readers developing research skills or looking for exciting sports content.

LERNER SPORTS FEATURES:
- Keyword search
- Topic navigation menus
- Fast facts
- Related bio suggestions to encourage more reading
- Admin view of reader statistics
- Fresh content updated regularly

and more!

Visit **LernerSports.com** for a free trial!

Lerner SPORTS

Copyright © 2022 by Lerner Publishing Group, Inc.

All rights reserved. International copyright secured. No part of this book may be reproduced, stored in a retrieval system, or transmitted in any form or by any means—electronic, mechanical, photocopying, recording, or otherwise—without the prior written permission of Lerner Publishing Group, Inc., except for the inclusion of brief quotations in an acknowledged review.

Lerner Publications Company
An imprint of Lerner Publishing Group, Inc.
241 First Avenue North
Minneapolis, MN 55401 USA

For reading levels and more information, look up this title at www.lernerbooks.com.

Main body text set in Myriad Pro Semibold.
Typeface provided by Adobe.

Designer: Mary Ross

Library of Congress Cataloging-in-Publication Data

Names: Leed, Percy, 1968– author.
Title: Peyton Manning : most valuable quarterback / Percy Leed.
Description: Minneapolis : Lerner Publications , [2022] | Series: Epic sports bios | Includes bibliographical references and index. | Audience: Ages 7–11 | Audience: Grades 4–6 | Summary: "Five-time MVP, two-time Super Bowl champion, and superstar quarterback Peyton Manning led the Indianapolis Colts and the Denver Broncos before retiring in 2016. Learn more about one of the NFL's most legendary players"— Provided by publisher.
Identifiers: LCCN 2020047869 (print) | LCCN 2020047870 (ebook) | ISBN 9781728404325 (library binding) | ISBN 9781728420509 (paperback) | ISBN 9781728418100 (ebook)
Subjects: LCSH: Manning, Peyton—Juvenile literature. | Football players—United States—Biography—Juvenile literature.
Classification: LCC GV939.M289 L44 2022 (print) | LCC GV939.M289 (ebook) | DDC 796.332092 [B]—dc23

LC record available at https://lccn.loc.gov/2020047869
LC ebook record available at https://lccn.loc.gov/2020047870

Manufactured in the United States of America
1-48490-49004-2/11/2021

TABLE OF CONTENTS

A SWEET VICTORY 4

FACTS AT A GLANCE 5

THE MANNING WAY 8

THE VOLUNTEER 12

COLTS CHAMPION 16

MOVE TO DENVER 20

SIGNIFICANT STATS 28
GLOSSARY 29
SOURCE NOTES 30
LEARN MORE 31
INDEX 32

A SWEET VICTORY

The Denver Broncos weren't supposed to beat the New England Patriots at the 2016 American Football Conference (AFC) Championship. The Patriots, led by quarterback Tom Brady, had a great offense. Many fans thought Broncos quarterback Peyton Manning was past his prime. Brady and Manning had clashed many times. This time, though, Manning seemed destined to lose.

Peyton Manning readies a pass during the 2016 AFC Championship game.

FACTS AT A GLANCE

Date of birth: March 24, 1976

Position: quarterback

League: National Football League (NFL)

Professional highlights: played four years of college football at the University of Tennessee; was the first starting quarterback to win a Super Bowl with two different teams; had 200 wins (including postseason games), the most of any NFL quarterback at the time

Personal highlights: has a brother Eli and father, Archie, who both played in the NFL; started the PeyBack Foundation in 1999 to support disadvantaged kids; became the father of twins, Marshall and Mosley, in 2011

But Manning wasn't ready to be counted out. Near the end of the first quarter he led an 83-yard drive to score Denver's first touchdown. The Broncos kept their lead the rest of the game. The team's strong defense shut down Brady's Patriots. Meanwhile, Manning stayed steady. He launched the quick, accurate passes he was known for.

Manning was 39 at the game, an age when most NFL players have already retired.

Manning and New England quarterback Tom Brady speak after the Broncos defeated the Patriots.

The Broncos held off the Patriots and claimed a 20–18 victory. Denver would take on the Carolina Panthers in the Super Bowl. "No question, this is a sweet day, this was a sweet victory," Manning said.

THE MANNING WAY

Peyton Williams Manning was born on March 24, 1976, in New Orleans, Louisiana. His father, Archie Manning, played quarterback for the New Orleans Saints and later for the Houston Oilers and Minnesota Vikings. Peyton seemed destined to be a football player. For him and his brothers, Cooper and Eli, the game was a way of life.

Archie Manning (*left*) played quarterback for the New Orleans Saints from 1971 to 1982.

FOOTBALL FAMILY

Following in their father's footsteps, Cooper, Peyton, and Eli all launched football careers. Cooper accepted a scholarship to the University of Mississippi (Ole Miss) but was forced to quit due to illness. Eli played for Ole Miss, then spent 16 seasons with the New York Giants.

Peyton and his brothers attended the Isidore Newman School in New Orleans. Peyton's football coaches quickly realized that he was special. He had natural talent and a great arm. He also had a deep understanding of the game.

By 10th grade, Peyton had taken over as Newman's varsity quarterback. His favorite receiver was his older brother, Cooper. Newman went 9–1 in the regular season. Then they went deep into the Louisiana state playoffs. By then, college scouts were getting a close look at both Manning boys. In his junior year, Peyton led Newman

From left: Archie, Peyton, Cooper, and Eli Manning

back to the playoffs. His senior year was even better. Peyton threw 39 touchdown passes and led Newman to an undefeated regular season.

Ole Miss fans assumed that Peyton would play there as his father had. But Peyton had a good feeling about the Tennessee Volunteers, called the Vols. He chose the University of Tennessee.

Manning in the Vols' locker room in 1996

THE VOLUNTEER

Manning worked hard to prove he deserved to be the Vols' starting quarterback. After a rocky first few games, he led the team to several big victories. The Vols earned a trip to the Gator Bowl, where they rolled to yet another victory against Virginia Tech. Manning was named Southeastern Conference (SEC) Freshman of the Year.

Manning dodges a defender in a 1995 game against the Kentucky Wildcats.

Manning throws a pass over a Kentucky defender.

Life was good for Tennessee fans during Manning's second year. The Vols lost only one game during the regular season. They quickly bounced back with an eight-game winning streak. A win in the Citrus Bowl capped off an amazing season. Manning had thrown for 2,954 yards and 22 touchdown passes. Tennessee finished ranked number 2 in the nation.

In Manning's third season was a game he'd been dreading for a long time. Tennessee would play Ole Miss, his dad's old team. "I sure didn't want to go down there in front of a lot of people . . . and play badly and lose, because I knew I'd never hear the end of it," he said.

Many fans were still angry that Manning hadn't picked Ole Miss, and they let him know it. But Manning's performance quickly shut down the crowd. He threw for 242 yards and a touchdown as Tennessee rolled to a 41–3 victory.

Manning celebrates a touchdown during the 1997 Citrus Bowl.

Neyland Stadium, Tennessee's home arena, full of fans for a game against Florida

The Vols finished the season with a 9–2 record. They returned to win the Citrus Bowl again. As the clock's final seconds ticked down, Tennessee fans stood and chanted "One more year! One more year!" Many expected Manning to leave college to enter the 1997 NFL Draft. But on March 5, he announced he would stay.

Manning didn't get the championship he wanted for his last season. But he led the Vols to an SEC title. He also broke two Tennessee records with 3,819 passing yards and 36 touchdowns. With college finished, he finally looked to the NFL.

COLTS CHAMPION

In 1998, the Indianapolis Colts chose Manning with their first draft pick. Manning and the Colts had a rough first season. They won just three games. After practicing hard over the off-season, Manning came back ready to win. He made it clear to his team that he wasn't going to settle for losing.

Manning holds up his Colts jersey at the 1998 NFL Draft.

GOAL-ORIENTED

Manning believes in setting and achieving goals. "I like to put [my goals] in writing so that afterward I can check the design against the finished product," he said.

By December, the Colts had won seven games in a row. Their winning streak kept going, launching them to a 13–3 record. The Colts were defeated in the playoffs. But the energy around the team had changed. In just one year, Manning had helped to transform the Colts into a Super Bowl favorite.

Manning led the Colts to the playoffs again the following year. In early 2001, he married his longtime girlfriend, Ashley Thompson. Things were going well, but Manning wanted greater success for his team. In 2002, the Colts hired a new coach to improve their weak defense.

The 2003 season was Manning's best yet. The Colts made it all the way to the AFC Championship game. They faced off against Tom Brady's Patriots. This time, the Patriots defense got the better of Manning and his receivers. The 2004 season opener gave the Colts a chance to get revenge on the Patriots. But they were bested again, losing 27–24.

Manning in a game against the San Diego Chargers

Manning's play continued to improve. In December, he broke the NFL single-season record for touchdown passes with 49. He was voted Most Valuable Player (MVP) for the season. But the Colts were cut down again by the Patriots in the playoffs. Some questioned Manning's ability to win big games. The questions only grew louder after the 2005 season. The Colts went 14–2 before losing to the underdog Pittsburgh Steelers in the playoffs.

The Colts faced the Patriots again in the 2006 AFC Championship game. By halftime the Colts were losing 21–6. Manning drove the Colts down the field and scored a touchdown on a quarterback sneak. Then Manning threw a quick pass for another touchdown. One two-point conversion later, the game was tied.

With a little more than five minutes left, New England had a three-point lead. After a few big passes and a New England penalty, the Colts had the ball at the 11-yard line. They went for the end zone and scored a touchdown with one minute left on the clock. New England couldn't recover. The Colts had done it. They'd beaten the Patriots and earned a trip to the Super Bowl.

The Colts were heavily favored to beat the Chicago Bears. Manning threw a 53-yard touchdown pass to help his team win 29–17. He had won his first Super Bowl.

Manning and Colts coach Tony Dungy after the Colts won the 2006 Super Bowl

MOVE TO DENVER

Manning led the Colts back to the Super Bowl in 2010. They lost to the New Orleans Saints 31–17. In 2011, he suffered neck problems that kept him out all season. On March 7, 2012, the Colts released him. Manning became a free agent for the 2012 season. That summer he made his first appearance with the Denver Broncos.

Manning throws a pass in one of his first games with the Denver Broncos.

FATHER FIGURE

Though Manning sat out the 2011 season, he did have a personal joy that year. His twins, Marshall and Mosley, were born.

Manning spent four strong seasons with Denver. In the 2013 season opener, he threw an amazing seven touchdowns. He was just the sixth player in NFL history to do so. Manning broke Brady's record for most touchdown passes in a season and Drew Brees's record for most passing

Manning calls a play in a 2012 game against the Cleveland Browns.

Manning and Broncos teammate Terrance Knighton celebrate Manning's record-breaking 509th touchdown pass in 2014.

yards in a season. He earned his fifth MVP award. He then led the Broncos to the Super Bowl, where they lost to the Seattle Seahawks. In 2014, Manning broke one of the biggest records yet. In a game against the San Francisco 49ers, he threw his 509th touchdown pass. The score made him the NFL's all-time leader.

Many fans had begun to wonder when Manning would retire. He struggled early in the 2015 season, missing several games due to a foot injury. But he had one more championship run in him.

Manning throws the ball in a game against the Kansas City Chiefs in 2015.

After besting the Patriots in the AFC Championship game, the Broncos defeated the Carolina Panthers in the Super Bowl. Manning became the first quarterback to lead two different teams to a Super Bowl victory. And the game was his 200th win, giving him the most wins of any starting quarterback in NFL history.

Manning holds up his second Super Bowl trophy.

Manning, his twin children, and some of his teammates after Manning announced his retirement from football

Manning announced his retirement in March 2016. As one of the NFL's most famous faces, he appears often in commercials. He spends time with other athletes and celebrities. He also uses his wealth for good. In 1999, he and his wife started the PeyBack Foundation to help support

Manning after handing out checks from the PeyBack Foundation in Denver

disadvantaged children. In 2007, St. Vincent Hospital in Indianapolis was renamed the Peyton Manning Children's Hospital. The new name honored Manning's work to help the hospital.

Some fans hope Manning will return to football as a TV announcer or buy an NFL team. Whatever he does next, it's clear that Manning will be successful at it, just as he was in nearly 20 seasons of pro football.

Manning announces his retirement in 2016.

SIGNIFICANT STATS

Won the regular-season MVP award five times

Won the Super Bowl twice

Won the 2007 Super Bowl MVP Award

Selected for the NFL Pro Bowl 14 times

Ranks third in NFL career passing touchdowns (539) and passing yards (71,940)

GLOSSARY

conference: one of two groups of teams (the AFC and the NFC) in the NFL

draft: when teams take turns choosing new players

free agent: a player who can sign with any team

off-season: the part of a year when a sports league is inactive

quarterback sneak: a quick run with the ball by the quarterback for short yardage

two-point conversion: advancing the ball across the goal line by running or catching a pass after a touchdown

varsity: the top team at a school

SOURCE NOTES

7 Jarrett Bell, "Bell: Broncos' Peyton Manning Isn't Done Yet after Epic Win over Tom Brady," *USA Today*, last modified January 25, 2016, https://www.usatoday.com/story/sports/nfl/columnist/bell/2016/01/24/peyton-manning-broncos-super-bowl-50-defense-tom-brady-patriots-afc-championship-game/79280020/.

14 Archie Manning and Peyton Manning, *Manning* (New York: HarperEntertainment, 2000), 113.

15 Manning and Manning, 115.

17 Manning and Manning, 349.

LEARN MORE

Booth, Tanis. *Football*. New York: AV2 by Weigl, 2020.

DK findout!: Football
https://www.dkfindout.com/us/sports/football/

Ducksters: Peyton Manning
https://www.ducksters.com/sports/peyton_manning.php

Kiddle: National Football League
https://facts.kiddle.co/National_Football_League

Levit, Joe. *Football's G.O.A.T.: Jim Brown, Tom Brady, and More*. Minneapolis: Lerner Publications, 2020.

Monson, James. *Behind the Scenes Football*. Minneapolis: Lerner Publications, 2020.

INDEX

Denver Broncos, 4, 6–7, 20, 22, 24

Indianapolis Colts, 16–20

Manning, Archie, 5, 8
Manning, Eli, 5, 8–9
MVP, 18, 22

New England Patriots, 4, 6–7, 17–19, 24

New Orleans, LA, 8–9, 20

quarterback, 4–5, 8–9, 12, 18, 24

record, 15, 17–18, 21, 22

Super Bowl, 5, 7, 17, 19–20, 22, 24

Tennessee Volunteers, 11–13, 15

PHOTO ACKNOWLEDGMENTS

Image credits: AP Photo/David Zalubowski, pp. 4, 7, 25; Mtsaride/Shutterstock.com, pp. 5, 28; AP Photo/Charlie Riedel, pp. 6, 8, 10; Doug Devoe/TSN/Icon SMI/Newscom, p. 11; AP Photo/Ed Reinke, pp. 12, 13; AP Photo/Scott Audette, p. 14; AP Photo/Wade Payne, p. 15; Al Messerschmidt Archive/ASSOCIATED PRESS, p. 16; AP Photo/Scott Boehm, p. 18; AP Photo/Chris O'Meara, p. 19; AP Photo/Greg Trott, pp. 20, 21, 24; AP Photo/Jack Dempsey, pp. 22, 26; Aaron M. Sprecher via AP, p. 23; Eric Bakke via AP, p. 27.

Cover: AP Photo/Scott Boehm.